Spies

by David Orme

Rans♦m

Trailblazers

Spies
by David Orme
Educational consultant: Helen Bird

Illustrated by Jan Martin

Published by Ransom Publishing Ltd.
51 Southgate Street, Winchester, Hants. SO23 9EH
www.ransom.co.uk

ISBN   978 184167 695 1

First published in 2009

Spies

Contents

Spies

Get the facts

What is spying?

You are the **Prime Minister** (or **President**). You find out that

- another country may be planning to do something that will harm your country.

- a group in your own country is planning to cause problems and commit crimes.

Who do you need?

You run a company making fizzy lemonade.

Another company invents a new lemonade with a secret recipe. It is the best lemonade ever!

You need to find out their secret, or your company will go bust!

Who do you need?

You need **A SPY** (sometimes known as **a Spook**.)

Spying is about finding out information from people who want to keep it secret. Spying is not always legal!

So you want to be a spook?

Which of these would make you a good spy?

 Good at martial arts and self defence

 Good-looking

 Calm in dangerous situations

 Good at disguise

 Ordinary-looking

 Good at driving cars really fast

 Good with technology

 Good at languages

 Walking around in a hat with SPY written on it

 Bad at keeping secrets

Useful tips to avoid being spied on.

Travel at busy times (you are harder to spot in a crowd).

Wear a hat with a big brim so CCTV cameras can't see your face.

Use a different route each time you travel.

Meet in the open, such as in a park.

SPY

Famous spying organisations

MI5 (MILITARY INTELLIGENCE – SECTION 5)

What do they do?

MI5 deals with security problems such as terrorist groups or organised crime inside the U.K.

MI5 HQ – Millbank, London

MI6 (MILITARY INTELLIGENCE – SECTION 6)

MI6 HQ – Vauxhall, London

What do they do?

They are in charge of U.K. spying operations in other countries.

FBI (FEDERAL BUREAU OF INVESTIGATION)

What do they do?

The FBI deals with major crimes across the whole of the United States.

FBI headquarters, Washington D.C.

CIA (THE CENTRAL INTELLIGENCE AGENCY)

What do they do?

They are in charge of American spying operations around the world.

*CIA Headquarters near Washington D.C.
– spooks just love tulips.*

KGB (COMMITTEE FOR STATE SECURITY)

What do they do?

Well, nothing anymore. The KGB was abolished in 1995.

The KGB dealt with security inside and outside the Soviet Union. They ran the much feared **secret police**.

The scary KGB headquarters in Moscow. No flowers here.

9

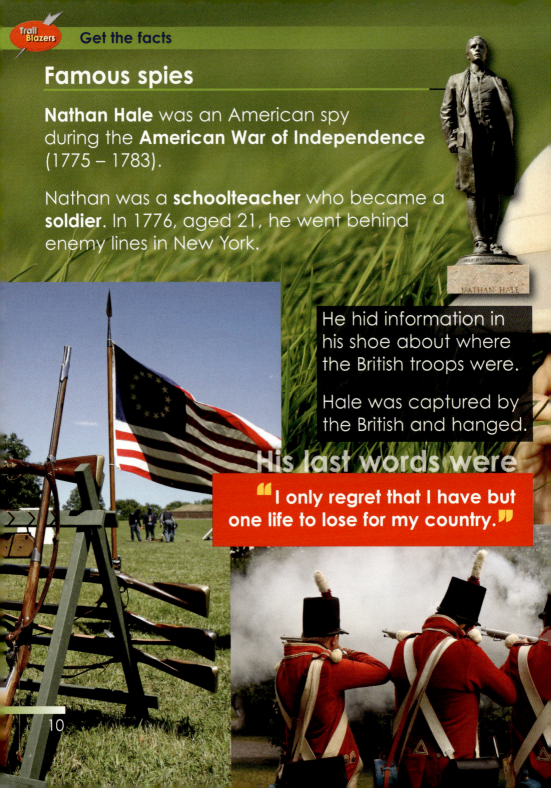

Famous spies

Nathan Hale was an American spy during the **American War of Independence** (1775 – 1783).

Nathan was a **schoolteacher** who became a **soldier**. In 1776, aged 21, he went behind enemy lines in New York.

He hid information in his shoe about where the British troops were.

Hale was captured by the British and hanged. His last words were

"I only regret that I have but one life to lose for my country."

NATHAN HALE

Robert Baden Powell

Robert Baden-Powell is best known for starting the boy scouts.

Before then he was a famous soldier. He fought in Africa during the **Boer War** (1899 – 1902).

He was clever at hiding information. He pretended to be interested in butterflies.

If he was caught, the enemy would never guess that this drawing of a butterfly ...

... was actually a **secret map** of a **fort**, showing the position of all the guns!

11

Secret codes

Passing **secret information** is an important part of a spy's work. They will often use **secret codes** so other people can't read the message.

Can you help the spy **crack the code**? It's going to be tricky – the code book has bullet holes in it!

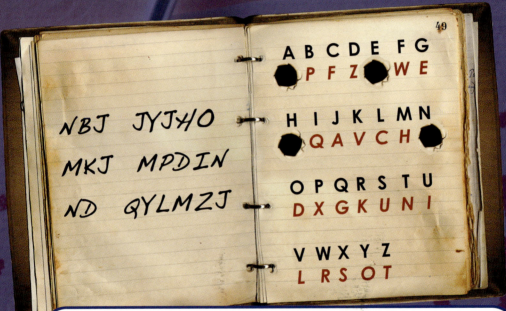

```
49

NBJ  JYJHO          A B C D E F G
MKJ  MPDIN           P F Z _ W E
ND  QYLMZJ          H I J K L M N
                    _ Q A V C H _
                    O P Q R S T U
                    D X G K U N I
                    V W X Y Z
                    L R S O T
```

This code adds in extra letters to muddle the message. Can you crack it?

Some People In Europe Say All Rabbits Eat Carrots Or Oranges Last.

Clue: look at the first letter of each word!

If someone can make up a code, someone else can crack it!

During the **Second World War**, Germany used this machine to create codes. It was called **ENIGMA**.

The messages were hard to crack because the code kept changing while the message was being sent.

They thought the messages could never be cracked.

The British code crackers were helped because operators sometimes made mistakes in sending messages.

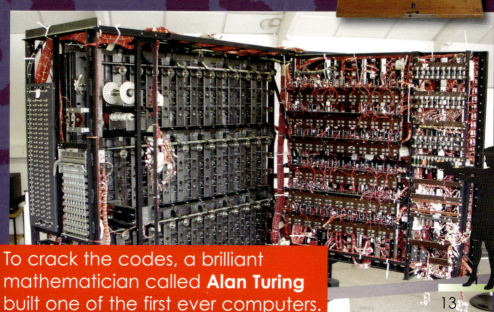

To crack the codes, a brilliant mathematician called **Alan Turing** built one of the first ever computers.

13

Brilliant spying gadgets

If you are a spy, you need to find out what other people are doing and saying – but they mustn't find out!

How do you do it?

 ## Plant a bug

A bug is a **microphone** plus a **radio**. It can be hidden anywhere so you can listen in to what people are saying.

You can disguise your bug to look like something else – here are some bugs!

Secret video cameras

So you think this is a fizzy drink can?

Wrong! It's a video camera!

Bugging phones and computers

Why not bug the phone or computer instead?

This looks harmless, but it can broadcast phone conversations.

Radio receivers can be used to pick up mobile phone calls.

Computer viruses called **spyware** can be sent to computers. Spies can then read other people's emails.

SO ARE THESE GADGETS LEGAL?

NO.

Even more brilliant spying gadgets

What if you need to keep an eye on someone outdoors?

This little plane is called a **Wasp**. It has a built-in camera for overhead spying.

But it's dark out here!

No problem! Try these night vision binoculars!

They've driven off! How do I track them?

Easy! Just stick this satellite tracking device to their car.

Are you being spied on?

Here are some ideas to help.

Before you start talking secrets, check out the room with this bug detector.

Think you are being followed? You need these rear view glasses. They have a little mirror at the side so you can see what's going on behind you.

The
Secret
Agent

Chapter 1:
The factory

The factory was well guarded, but there was a way to get inside. It was risky, but Shane had agreed to try. He was a new member of the protest group.

'I was in the army once,' Shane told the group. 'I did under-cover operations. It's what I'm good at.'

If he could steal some important papers, the protest group could show the world what the government was doing in the factory.

Shane clipped the wire fence and crept silently through the trees. There was an alarm, but Shane knew how to deal with that.

He took a tool from his backpack and forced open the window. He slipped inside the room and pulled down the blind.

The light went on in the room. Sitting at the desk was Colonel Redman, head of secret intelligence.

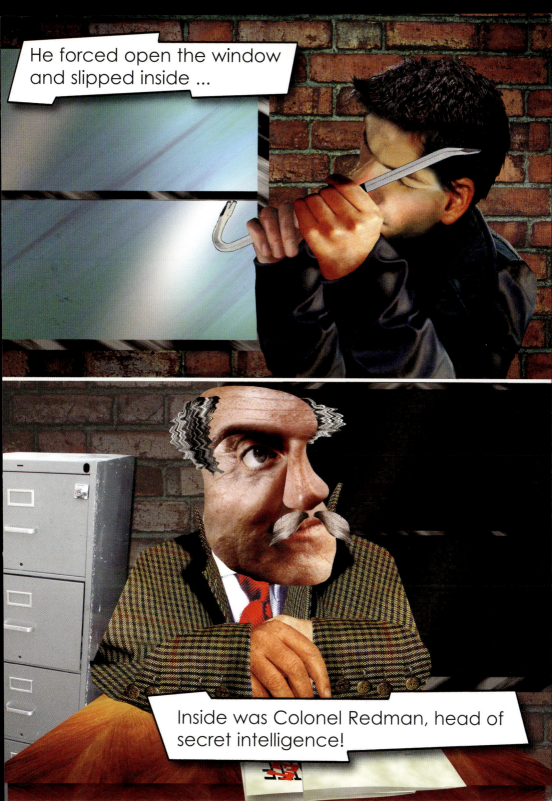

Chapter 2:
The file

'Well done, Mike,' said Colonel Redman. 'It's all working out fine.'

Shane was the name Mike Fury used when he joined the protest group. None of the group had any idea he was a government agent.

'We've made up the fake papers,' Colonel Redman had told Mike. 'They are in this file. If they send this information to the newspapers, they will end up looking really stupid when we prove them wrong.'

Mike picked up the file. Next to it on the desk was another file. 'Skylonite production – top secret.'

'Don't take them that one!' said Colonel Redman. 'That really would give them something to protest about!'

Mike nodded. He had learnt that in his job you didn't ask questions. If you didn't know anything, no one could force the information out of you – even if you were tortured.

Chapter 3:
The group

The next day Mike, pretending to be Shane, met up with the group. They always met up in a different place each time. That way, no one could bug them.

Mike handed the file to Seb, the group leader.

'Brilliant Job, Shane! When we go public on this, the government will be forced to shut that evil factory down!'

'When will you send the copies out?'

'Friday. We want this to be a big story in the Sunday papers.'

'Take care, Shane. You know what the intelligence service is like. If they find out it was you, you'll end up in prison on a made-up charge. Then you'll be found dead in your cell. They'll say it was suicide.'

Oh no they won't, thought Mike. And thanks for the information. Colonel Redman will find that really useful!

But something was worrying Mike.

Chapter 4:
Mike does some research

Mike remembered the file at the factory, and what Colonel Redman had said.

'Don't take them that one! That really would give them something to protest about!'

Skylonite. What could it be?

Mike did some research on the Internet. He was really shocked. Could the government really be making stuff like that?

There was only one thing for it. He had to join the protest group – for real!

When Mike got to the meeting, the group was waiting for him. He was grabbed from behind. Seb waved the file Mike had given them under his nose.

'This just didn't check out. So I checked *you* out, Shane – or is it Mike?'

'Believe me, Seb, I'm on your side!' shouted Mike desperately. 'I came to tell you that I'm working for you from now on.'

The group laughed.

'Do you expect us to believe that?'

The group closed in. They knew how to deal with traitors.

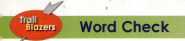

Spies word check

bugging	mathematician
CCTV	microphone
code crackers	protest group
colony	qualities
count	receiver
disguise	security
equipment	steganography
foreign	tattooed
gadget	technology
government	terrorist
information	tortured
intelligence	traitor
legal	under-cover
martial arts	